Use these stickers to make your own
Brewster at the end of the book

BRAKING
BREWSTER

Bath New York Singapore Hong Kong Cologne Delhi Melbourne

One morning, Vee had an exciting job for Brewster and Wilson.
"It's training time!" said Wilson, excitedly.

Brewster hoped they would be back in time to practise the new moves he learned yesterday.

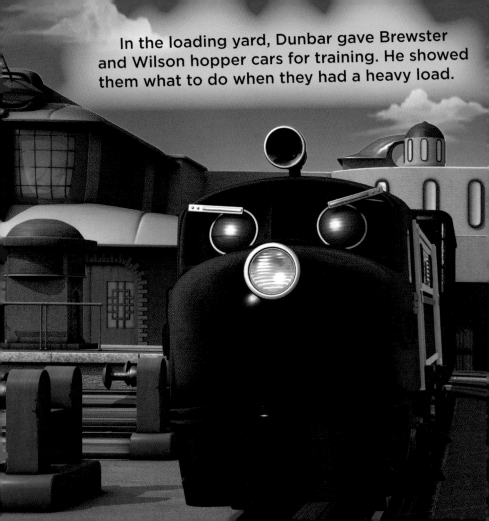

In the loading yard, Dunbar gave Brewster and Wilson hopper cars for training. He showed them what to do when they had a heavy load.

Wilson found it really hard at first – but he kept trying. Then he did it!

The two chuggers were ready to start their journey. Dunbar warned them that it was harder going downhill with a heavy load, so they must come back slowly.

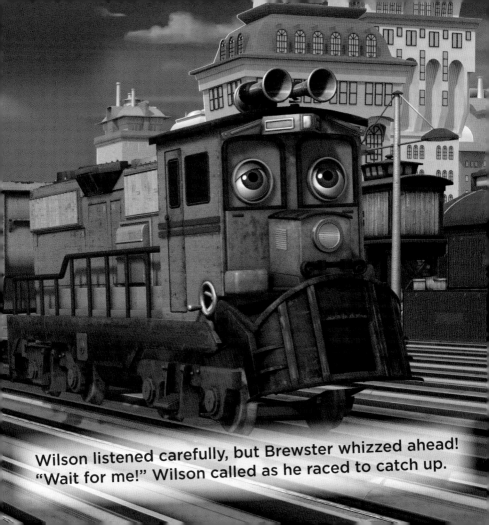

Wilson listened carefully, but Brewster whizzed ahead! "Wait for me!" Wilson called as he raced to catch up.

Vee told the chuggers to go to the mountain quarry to collect some stone. They were to take the left tunnel at the mountain.

On the platform next to them, Morgan the mechanic suddenly slipped over on some oil. Wilson watched as Morgan sprinkled sand over the oil so his feet could grip.

When Brewster and Wilson came out of the tunnel and looked up at the mountain they saw it was a very long way away.

They climbed the track, higher and higher up the mountain. Suddenly there were two tunnels in front of them.

Wilson couldn't remember what tunnel they had to take. He wished he'd listened more carefully to Vee, but he thought they needed the right one.

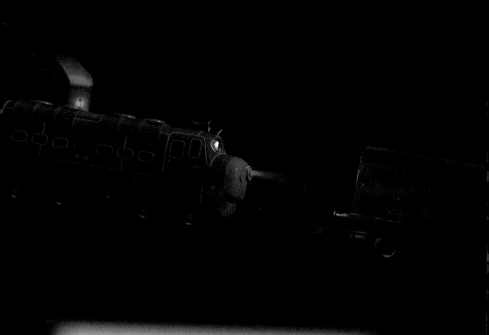

Before long, the tracks began to slope downwards.

"Honking horns! We're going downhill!" said Brewster, worriedly.

They were going the wrong way! After turning around, they rushed back uphill and chose the tunnel on the left this time.

At the quarry, Karen, loaded stones into Wilson's hopper car. Wilson struggled to keep his doors shut so Brewster offered to go first.

But when it was Wilson's turn, there was only dust left!

Brewster zoomed ahead. "Downhill's easy peasy," he said.

Suddenly, the track became too steep and Brewster lost control!

"My brakes don't work. Help!" he cried.

"HELP!"

Wilson had a great idea. He whizzed ahead of Brewster and dropped his load of stone dust on the track,

"Brake on the dust!" Wilson called.

It worked!
They both slowed down
and came to a stop.

The two chuggers made their way back to the depot.

Tick a box when you spot each difference!

1 2 3 4 5

Can you help Wilson and Brewster find the right track to the quarry?

Can you match these colours to the characters from the story?

blue green aqua

Can you tell which chugger has been mixed up?